The Berenstain Bears
and the
BIG BLOOPER

Cubs learn new words
every day —
including some that
they should not say!

A First Time Book®

The Berenstain Bears and the BIG BLOOPER

Stan & Jan Berenstain

Random House 🏠 New York

Copyright © 2000 by Berenstain Enterprises, Inc. All rights reserved under International and
Pan-American Copyright Conventions. Published in the United States by Random House, Inc.,
New York, and simultaneously in Canada by Random House of Canada Limited, Toronto.

www.randomhouse.com/kids www.berenstainbears.com

Library of Congress Cataloging-in-Publication Data
Berenstain, Stan, 1923–
The Berenstain Bears and the big blooper / Stan & Jan Berenstain.
p. cm. SUMMARY: When she spills her milk, Sister Bear uses a new word she heard on a
video, and a surprised Mama Bear explains to her that some words are not polite to use.
ISBN 0-679-88962-0 (trade) — ISBN 0-679-98962-5 (lib. bdg.)
[1. Bears—Fiction. 2. Etiquette—Fiction. 3. Swearing—Fiction.]
I. Berenstain, Jan, 1923– . II. Title.
PZ7.B4483 Bejji 2000 [Fic]—dc21 00-44532

Printed in the United States of America October 2000 10 9 8 7 6 5 4 3 2 1

RANDOM HOUSE and colophon are registered trademarks of Random House, Inc.

Sister Bear was just beginning
to wonder what to do with herself
one afternoon when the phone rang.

It was Lizzy Bruin asking
her to come over to play.

"Bring your dolls with you,"
said Lizzy. "We'll play house.
And, later on, we can watch a
video."

"Great!" said Sister. "I'll
check with my mom and be
right over."

A visit to Lizzy's house was perfectly all right with Mama Bear. In fact, she had a lot of gardening to do that afternoon. Sister and Lizzy were always a pleasure to have around, but if they played over at Lizzy's that afternoon, Mama could get more work done.

Sister put her dolls in their stroller
and hurried over to Lizzy's.

Lizzy was waiting for her at the door and helped her carry the dolls upstairs to her room. Sister and Lizzy had been playing house with their dolls the last time Sister visited, so they just picked up where they left off.

Sister's doll Amanda had been
pestering her mother—played by
Lizzy's doll Christie—to let her
bake cookies in the kitchen.

"Now, Amanda," said Christie—
it was really Lizzy's voice—"you
know I have a lot of work to do
around the house. I don't have
time to help you bake cookies."

"Aw, gee, Mom!" whined
Amanda—it was Sister's voice—
"I *never* get to bake cookies. You
never let me do anything!"

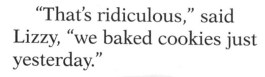

"That's ridiculous," said
Lizzy, "we baked cookies just
yesterday."

"But I want to bake cookies now!"
shouted Sister, getting into her role.

"Stop that shouting!"
yelled Lizzy. "Don't speak
to me in that tone of
voice. You'll be sent to
your room in another
minute!"

Before Sister could yell back and get sent to her room, Lizzy's mother came to the door. She looked a little frazzled.

"What's all the shouting about?" she asked. "I'm trying to make some phone calls and I don't need all this commotion."

"We're just playing, Mom," said Lizzy.
"Can't you do something quieter?" sighed her mom.
"Can we watch a video?" asked Lizzy.
"I suppose so," agreed her mother, heading back downstairs.

Lizzy and Sister brought their dolls into the
family room and settled down in front of the TV.

"Hey, look!" said Lizzy.
"Here's that video that
Barry rented." Barry was
Lizzy's older brother.
"Let's watch that."
"Okay," agreed Sister.

The video was called *Trouble at Big Bear High,* and it looked pretty grown-up. It was all about teenagers in high school.

Sister didn't understand a lot of it.

The teenagers in the video got angry and upset with each other, and Sister didn't always understand why.

They teased each other and made fun of each other's clothes.

They used a lot of words that Sister didn't understand. Whenever the teenagers got angry or upset, they said words that Sister had never heard before. She figured that these words were sort of like "Phooey!" or "Fudge!" but more grown-up.

She whispered one or two to herself. They sounded pretty good.

When the video was over, Sister and Lizzy played with their dolls some more, then went outside to ride bikes. Finally, it was time for Sister to go home for supper. She gathered her dolls together and headed home, thinking about the video she had seen. She wasn't sure whether she liked it or not.

At the table, Sister began to tell Papa, Mama, and Brother about the video. She told them about Big Bear High and about how teenagers there got angry and upset and teased each other and made fun of each other's clothes.

"That's very interesting," said Mama, not paying too much attention. She was busy with baby Honey and Papa was already busy eating.

But Brother looked up. "I saw that video with Barry," he said. "Did you like it? Isn't it a little *old* for you?"

"No!" said Sister, offended. "I liked it a lot. I thought it was great!" She waved her hand to show how great it was and knocked over her glass of milk. It spilled all over the table.

Sister was about to say "Oh, phooey!"
or "Oh, fudge!" But one of the words
from the video popped into her head,
and she said it real loud!

There was a pause. Mama, Papa, and Brother stared at her with their mouths open.

Uh-oh, thought Sister.

"*What* did you say?" gasped Mama.

"Um...," mumbled Sister. "I forget."

Papa was speechless. He just sat there
with his fork halfway to his mouth. Brother
was turning away, trying not to laugh.

"Where in the world did you get *that*
from?" asked Mama, folding her arms.

"W-w-well...," stammered Sister, and it all came out—all about Lizzy's mom having to make some phone calls and about finding the video Barry rented and about the grown-up words Sister hadn't heard before.

"I see," said Mama thoughtfully. "I have to tell you, Sister, that the words you heard on that video are not nice words. They are words that no cub should *ever* use at any time. I don't care how angry or upset they are."

"Do grownups ever use those words?" asked Sister. Brother snorted, trying to hold in a laugh.

Mama looked at Papa. "Ahem!" she said.

"What? Huh?" said Papa, coming out of his trance. "Oh, yes! Well, Sister, sometimes, once in a while, grownups do use words like those—like when they hit their thumbs with a hammer or when they stub their toes real bad or when they run the hose over with the lawn mower or when the kicker muffs a field goal or…"

"That's quite enough, thank you," said Mama firmly. "The point is that nobody, not even adults and *certainly* not cubs, should use words like those at all. They're simply not nice. Now, let's clean the milk up off the table."

Later, when Sister was getting tucked into bed, she thought of something. "Mama...," she said. "If those words from the video are not nice, then why do cubs and grownups use them?" Mama sat down at the edge of the bed and sighed.

"Because," she said, "it's easy. It's an easy way to seem grown-up, it's an easy way to get attention. And," she added, "after a while, it gets to be a habit—a bad habit."

"Sister," said Mama.
"Yes, Mama," said Sister. Her eyes were closing.
"Does all that make sense, dear?" said Mama.
But Sister was fast asleep.